Bats to the Rescue!

adapted by Veronica Paz
based on the screenplay "Freddie the Fruit Bat Saves Halloween"
written by Rosemary Contreras
illustrated by Art Mawhinney

Simon Spotlight/Nickelodeon
New York   London   Toronto   Sydney

Based on the TV series *Go, Diego, Go!*™ as seen on Nick Jr.™

SIMON SPOTLIGHT
An imprint of Simon & Schuster Children's Publishing Division
1230 Avenue of the Americas, New York, New York 10020
© 2010 Viacom International Inc. All rights reserved.
NICK JR., *Go, Diego, Go!*, and all related titles, logos, and characters are trademarks of Viacom International Inc.
All rights reserved, including the right of reproduction in whole or in part in any form.
SIMON SPOTLIGHT and colophon are registered trademarks of Simon & Schuster, Inc.
For information about special discounts for bulk purchases, please contact Simon & Schuster Special Sales at
1-866-506-1949 or business@simonandschuster.com.
Manufactured in the United States of America 0610 LAK
First Edition
2 4 6 8 10 9 7 5 3 1
ISBN 978-1-4424-0228-7

¡Hola! I'm Diego, and this is my sister Alicia! We're Animal Rescuers. Today is Halloween, and we're having a party! Do you know what Alicia and I are dressed up as? *¡Sí!* I'm dressed as a bat, and Alicia is a butterfly! What do you like to dress up as on Halloween?

We're setting up trick-or-treating booths for our Halloween party. Each booth will have its own special treat. Alicia's booth will have tasty fruit, and my booth will have yummy chocolate. What is your favorite Halloween treat?

We're almost done decorating for the party. We can't wait for everyone to arrive, especially Linda the Llama. She and the baby llamas are bringing all of the treats for the party.

Look! It's our friend Freddie the Fruit Bat! Freddie loves Halloween. That's because Halloween is celebrated at night. Fruit bats sleep all day and stay up all night. I'm dressed as a bat because I love Halloween night, too!

Oh, no! I hear animals in trouble! My special camera, Click, can help us find the animals that need our help. Say "Click!" Wow! Click is all dressed up for Halloween too.

Click says that the animals in trouble are tall, with soft fur, and can carry lots of stuff on their backs. Click can zoom through the forest to find the animals. Will you help? Great!

These first animals are small, live in the water, and say, "Quack, quack, quack!" Are they the animals in trouble? No! They are ducks dressed up as pumpkins! Let's keep looking!

Could these be our animals? They look tall and seem to be carrying a lot. Yes, it's a match! It's Linda the Llama . . . and the baby llamas dressed up as clowns! They can't get to the party because the bridge is broken. The little llamas will be so sad if they can't come to the party. And we won't be able to trick-or-treat without the treats! We need to fix the bridge to save Halloween. Will you help Freddie and me? Great! Bats to the rescue!

To get to the broken bridge, we have to find a way through this maze. The sign shows that some of the paths are blocked, but we don't know which ones. How will we find our way through? Freddie says we can make it through the maze by listening for echoes.

Yeah! If Freddie makes a sound, and the sound hits a wall, then the sound will bounce back. That sound is an echo, and it means the path is blocked. We need to find the path where the sound doesn't bounce back. Which path should we take?

¡Muy bien! We used echoes to find the right path and made it through the maze! Freddie says that from way up in the sky the maze looks like something you see on Halloween. What does it look like? *¡Sí!* A jack-o'-lantern!

It's Baby Jaguar! He says his blue hat for his costume is stuck in this tree hole, and he's too big to go in and get it. But Freddie is small enough to fly into the tree hole. Go, Freddie, go!

It's pretty dark in the tree hole. Good thing bats have really good eyesight and can see in the dark. Look! Freddie found three different hats in the tree hole. Which is Baby Jaguar's blue hat?

Great job finding the hat! Now Baby Jaguar's costume is complete! He makes a great pirate. *Argh!* Baby Jaguar is going to the Animal Rescue Center to help Alicia with the party. The animals can't wait to start trick-or-treating. Freddie and I have to go help the llamas and fix the bridge. Let's go, *amigos*!

We have to go through this tunnel to get to the broken bridge. Lead the way, Freddie! Wait! What's that sound?

¡Fantasmas! Ghosts! Could they be real? No! It's just the Bobo Brothers dressed up as ghosts. That was a good trick, Bobos! But we can't stop and play. We have to save the Halloween party!

To get to the broken bridge we have to keep going down this path. *¡Cuidado!* Watch out for spiderwebs! We don't want to bump into them and ruin them. Mr. Spider says we just have to figure out what the webs look like to get past them.

What does the first spiderweb look like? *¡Sí!* A bat, just like Freddie and me! What do the other spiderwebs look like? Yeah! A spider and a ghost! Thank you for helping us make it past the spiderwebs!

We're at the broken bridge. Linda and the baby llamas are on the other side and can't cross it! Look! The rope holding up the bridge broke. To fix the bridge we need someone to fly over and tie the broken ends of the rope together. Do you know someone who can fly? Yeah! Freddie! To help Freddie fly to the other side of the bridge and bring the rope back, we have to say "fly" in Spanish. In Spanish we say "*vuela.*" Say *"¡Vuela!"*

Yeah, we did it! The bridge is fixed! Come on, everyone! Let's get back to the party!

Now that we have the treats, it's time to celebrate Halloween! Freddie loves the booths with fruit treats. Can you guess why? *¡Correcto!* Fruit bats love to eat fruit! Yum! What a treat!

Freddie saved Halloween! But Freddie couldn't have done it without your help. Put your arms out to your sides to fly like a fruit bat! Flap, flap, flap! Bats to the rescue! Happy Halloween, everyone!

Did you know?

Just Like You . . .

Bats might have wings and be able to fly like birds, but they're actually mammals, just like people, dogs, and cats.

What's in a Name?

Fruit bats get their name from their diet—they eat lots of flower nectar and fruits.

What a Cape!

The Livingstone's fruit bat is one of the world's largest fruit bats; its wingspan can be up to six feet wide!

Night Creatures

Bats are nocturnal which means that they sleep most of the day and are active at night.